DEX
The Heart of a Hero

DEX
The Heart of a Hero

Caralyn Buehner   illustrated by **Mark Buehner**

HARPERCOLLINS*PUBLISHERS*

In memory of
Roger Buehner,
a hero

Dex: The Heart of a Hero
Text copyright © 2004 by Caralyn Buehner
Illustrations copyright © 2004 by Mark Buehner

This 2009 edition licensed for publication by Barnes & Noble, Inc., by arrangement with HarperCollins Publishers.

HarperCollins Publishers® is a registered trademark.

Barnes & Noble, Inc.
122 Fifth Avenue
New York, NY 10011

ISBN 978-1-4351-1641-2
Manufactured in China.
05 06 07 08 09 MCH 10 9 8 7 6 5 4 3 2 1

Dexter was a little dog. His legs were little, his tail was little, his body was little. He looked like a plump sausage sitting on four little meatballs.

Being the size that he was, Dex was often overlooked. The other dogs grew tired of waiting for Dex to catch up when they played chase, and after a while they forgot to invite him at all. No one really seemed to notice him, except when Cleevis, the tomcat, demonstrated how he could stand right over Dex and not even ruffle his fur.

Yes, everything about Dex was little—except for his dreams.

He wanted to be a HERO. He could just *see* it.

THE MIGHTY DEX FLEW UP INTO THE DARK AND STARRY NIGHT. . . .

But *wanting* and *being* are two different things. Dex lived on dreams until one day, after crawling out from under Cleevis yet again, he decided there had to be more to life than gazing at the underside of a cat. There had to be more to *him*. If he *could* be a hero, he *would*!

So Dex started training. He read every superhero comic book he could find. He watched every hero movie ever made. He went to the library.

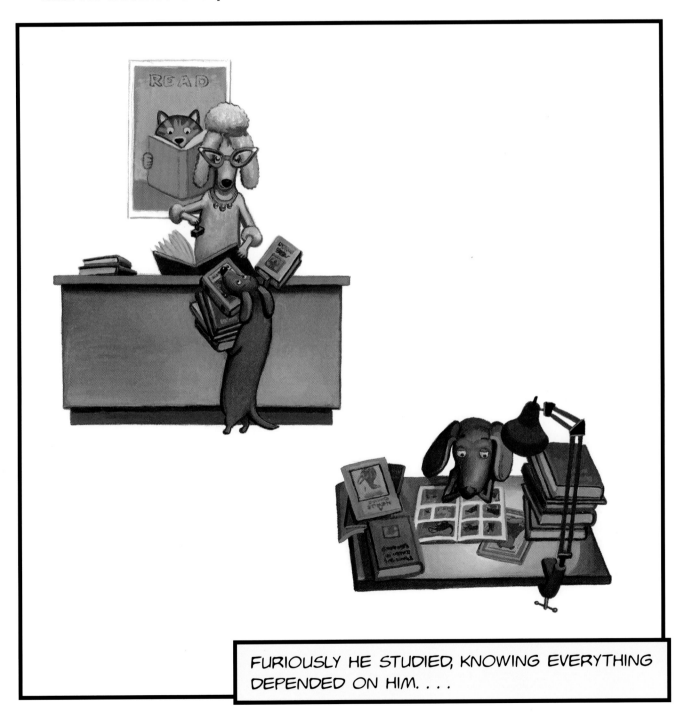

FURIOUSLY HE STUDIED, KNOWING EVERYTHING DEPENDED ON HIM. . . .

Dex figured that a hero must have strong muscles.

He needed exercise, and lots of it!

Dex started trotting to the corner and back every morning.

He hopped over every crack in the sidewalk.

He struggled to climb the garbage pile: up and over and down, then up and over and down again. All day long he worked, day after day. Even at bedtime, when he wanted to flop on the rug with his tongue hanging out, Dex forced himself to circle five extra times.

THE MIGHTY DEX PRESSED ON, THROUGH WIND AND RAIN AND STORM AND FATIGUE. . . .

When it got easier to run to the corner and back, Dex did it again, and then again. Then he dragged a sock filled with sand as he ran, then *two* socks. When Cleevis was bored and stood in the middle of the sidewalk to block his way, Dex dropped to the ground and slid right under him. He was too busy to be bothered by Cleevis.

Dex was tired; he was sore. He was working so hard that he almost forgot what he was working for. But one night, as he dragged himself to bed after his last set of push-ups, Dex stopped in front of the mirror and flexed. He could feel them! He could see them! Muscles!

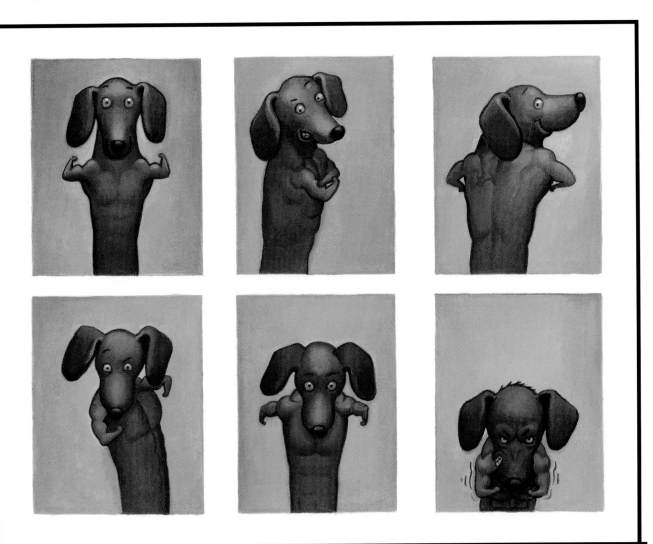

FASTER THAN A ROLLING BALL, STRONGER THAN THE TOUGHEST RAWHIDE, ABLE TO LEAP TALL FENCES IN A SINGLE BOUND!

Now Dex didn't "take" the stairs—he skimmed them! He leaped over hydrants; he vaulted up curbs. He could jump over the garbage mountain without touching the top! He could run like the wind; he felt as if his legs had springs!

Only one thing was missing.

Finally, a small brown package arrived. Dex ripped it open.

His HERO suit! It was red, with a shiny green cape, and it fit like a glove. Dex loved the way it felt, he loved the way it looked, and he loved the feeling he had when he put it on.

He was ready.

WITH THE COURAGE OF A LION, THE STRENGTH OF A BEAR, AND THE HEART OF A HERO . . .

When Dex went out in his suit for the very first time, he looked up the street and down. He noticed a young pup trying to cross the street. Dex sprang into action.

"May I help you?" he asked. He guided the wide-eyed pup across the street and grinned as the pup stared up at him with its mouth hanging open. The pup whispered, "Wow! It's Super Dog!"

SUPER DOG. Dex liked the sound of that.

Of course, when Cleevis saw Dex, he just had to comment.

"Hey Dex, where's the party?" And when he saw him a few days later, Cleevis called out, "Look, everybody! It must be Halloween. Anybody got a treat for Dex?"

Dex was so busy that he was able to ignore Cleevis—for the most part. The only time his face even got red was when Cleevis yelled, "Where'd you get that dress-up?" Dex had to wonder if Cleevis saw anything but the suit. Didn't he understand that the suit was just a way to let people know he was there to help?

THE SUN GLINTED OFF OF HIS EMERALD CAPE AS SUPER DOG RACED TO THE RESCUE. . . .

There was a mouse he saved from a sewer,

a purse snatcher he tackled;

he fixed his neighbor's sprinkler;

he found a lost kitten,

pulled a rat away from a live wire,

tracked down a lost wallet,

put out a trash fire,

and organized a neighborhood cleanup day.

It seemed that now, whenever anyone needed help, they turned to Dex, and Dex had never been happier.

Late one evening there was a banging at the door. When Dex answered, it seemed as if the whole neighborhood was yipping and yeowling in a panic.

"It's Cleevis!" they shouted. "He's stuck in a tree. Hurry, Dex, hurry!"

Dex raised his eyebrows. It was not like Cleevis to move enough to get into any trouble.

In a flash he was dressed and ready.

IT WAS CLEARLY A DESPERATE SITUATION. . . .

As he got closer, Dex could see Cleevis. He had been chasing a squirrel to the top of the tree, but had slipped and was hanging by one claw from a slender branch.

"I'm slipping!" Cleevis screeched. "Help me!"

Dex looked desperately around for something to climb on. There were no boxes or ladders, not even any trash cans. Then Dex looked at the crowd.

"Quick, everybody!" Dex shouted. "I've got an idea!" Dex leaped onto the end of the teeter-totter facing the tree, pushing it to the ground.

"Everybody on the other end! One! Two! Three!!!!"

All the animals jumped together on the other end of the teeter-totter, catapulting Dex into the air. He soared over the crowd, his ears and cape streaming out behind him. . . .

THE MIGHTY DEX FLEW UP INTO THE DARK AND STARRY NIGHT. . . .

Dex scrambled onto the branch next to Cleevis. Quickly he pulled off his cape and tied its four corners onto the screeching cat.

"Jump!" Dex shouted. "Jump, Cleevis!"

With an ear-piercing shriek, Cleevis let go. The billowing cape caught the air and parachuted the big cat to the ground. Dex backed up and slid to the ground amidst the cheers of the crowd.

Dex was bruised and tired, but he forgot his discomfort as Cleevis

sheepishly lumbered over, still tangled in the green cape.

"Thanks, Dex. You really are a hero!"

Dex didn't think he could feel any better, but he did—just a little—the next day, when Cleevis sidled up next to him and whispered, "Say, Dex, could I be your partner?"

Dex looked the big tomcat up and down. It would take a *lot* of work to turn Cleevis into a hero. He could hardly wait.

"Sure," said Dex with a grin. "Sure."

WITH TWICE THE BRAINS AND TRIPLE THE BRAWN, OUR HEROES FORGE ON, EVER READY TO LEND A HELPING PAW!